Wild About Books

by JUDY SIERRA

pictures by MARC BROWN

F
FRANCES LINCOLN
CHILDREN'S BOOKS

It started the summer of 2002,
When the Springfield librarian, Molly McGrew,
By mistake drove her bookmobile into the zoo.
Molly opened the door and she let down the stair,
Turned on the computer and sat on her chair.

At first all the animals watched from a distance,
But Molly could conquer the strongest resistance.

By reading aloud from the good Dr. Seuss,
She quickly attracted a mink and a moose,
A wombat, an oryx, a lemur, a lynx,
Eight elephant calves and a family of skinks.

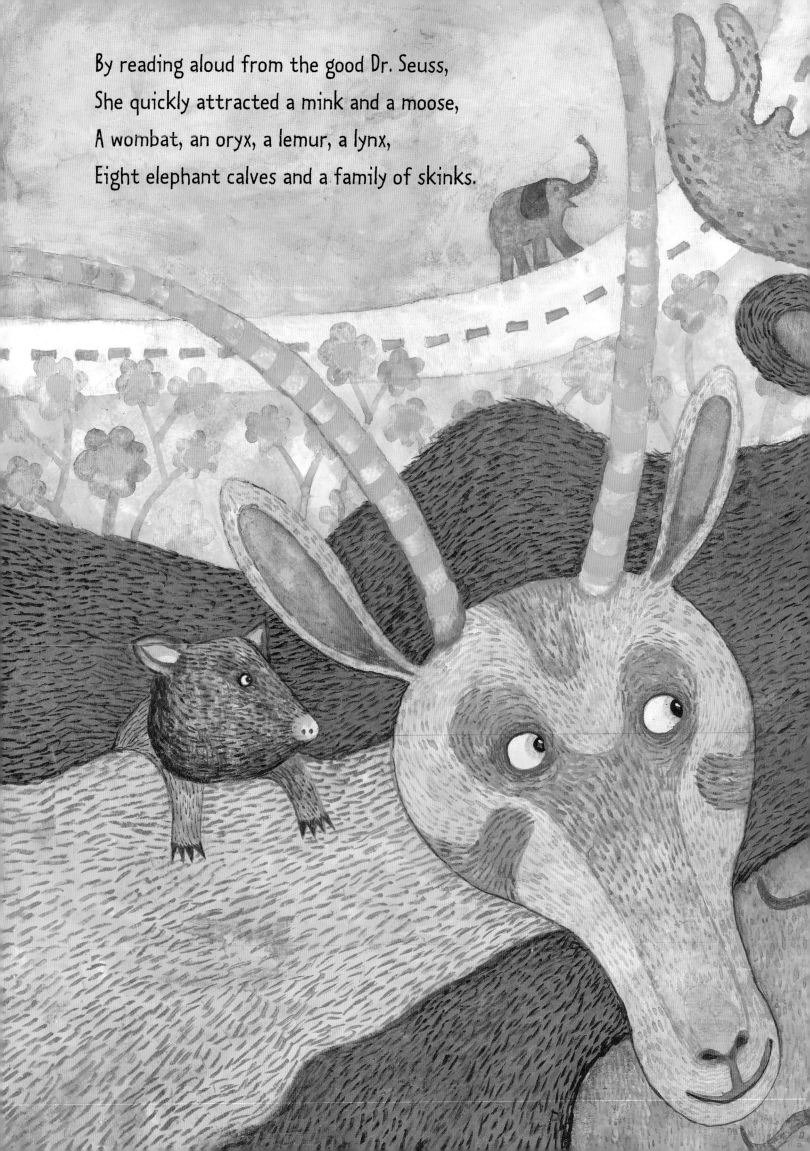

In a flash, every beast in the zoo was stampeding
To learn all about this new something called reading.

Forsaking their niches, their nests, and their nooks,
They went wild, simply wild, about wonderful books,
Choosing thin books and fat books and **Cat in the Hat** books
And new books and true books and heaps of how-to books.

Giraffes wanted tall books and crickets craved small books,
While geckos could only read stick-to-the-wall books.

The pandas demanded more books in Chinese.
Molly filled their requests, always eager to please.
She even found waterproof books for the otter,
Who never went swimming without **Harry Potter**.

Raccoons read alone and baboons read in bunches.
And llamas read dramas while eating their llunches.

Hyenas shared jokes with the red-bellied snakes,
And they howled and they hissed till their funny bones ached.

A tree kangaroo, who adored **Nancy Drew**,
Began solving mysteries right there at the zoo,
Such as, why were the bandicoot's books overdue?

Gently, Molly taught lessons in treating books right,
For the boa constrictor squeezed **Crictor** too tight,
Baby bunnies mucked up **Goodnight Moon** with their paws,
Giant termites devoured **The Wizard of Oz**,

And bears' love of books was completely outrageous –
They licked all the pictures right off all the pages.

BIG BAD
BRUCE

Tasmanian devils found books so exciting

That soon they had given up fighting for writing.

They made up adventures so thrilling and new

That the others decided to be authors, too.

Pythons wrote with their tails, penguins wrote with their bills,

And porcupines wrote with their very own quills.

At the new insect zoo, bugs were scribbling haiku.
(The scorpion gave each a stinging review.)

It was a dark and stormy night. The wind howled. The moon cast a mournful pale yellow glow. bogs waited in the

As the cheetah's new novel began to take shape,
He read chapters each night to the Barbary ape;
And although the gazelle couldn't spell very well,
Like everyone else, she had stories to tell.

Imagine the hippo's enormous surprise
When her memoir was given the Zoolitzer Prize.

With so many new books, Molly knew what to do –
She hired twelve beavers, a stork, and a gnu
To build a branch library there at the zoo.
Then the animals cried, "We can do it ourselves!
We can check the books out. We can put them on shelves."

And they did, and they do, up to this very day.
Three cheers for the Zoobrary–

Hip, hip, hooray!

When you visit the zoo now, you surely won't mind
If the animals seem just a bit hard to find –
They are snug in their niches, their nests, and their nooks,
Going wild, simply wild, about wonderful books.

Would you like to read any of the stories that
drove the animals simply wild about wonderful books?
Here are a few of the animals' favourites:

The Cat in the Hat by Dr. Seuss
Crictor by Tomi Ungerer
Goodnight Moon by Margaret Wise Brown
The Harry Potter series by J.K. Rowling
The Nancy Drew series by Carolyn Keene
The Wizard of Oz by L. Frank Baum

Text copyright © Judy Sierra 2004
Illustrations copyright © Marc Brown 2004. All Rights Reserved.
First published in the USA in 2004 by Alfred A. Knopf,
an imprint of Random House Children's Books.
Published by arrangement with Random House Children's Books,
a division of Random House, Inc. New York, USA. All Rights Reserved.

First published in Great Britain in 2006 by
Frances Lincoln Children's Books, 4 Torriano Mews,
Torriano Avenue, London NW5 2RZ

www.franceslincoln.com

British Library Cataloguing in Publication Data available on request

ISBN 10: 1-84507-526-9
ISBN 13: 978-1-84507-526-2

Printed in China

135798642

This book is for our favourite doctor,
artist, poet, fun concocter:
Theodor Seuss Geisel, 1904–1991.

Judy Sierra and Marc Brown